Return to Glory or Journey to Disaster

The corridor pulses with an eerie glow that comes from a doorway at o█████d that shimmers like a thousand light█████ Wisps of cloud reach out like s█████████ as if to grab you in their █

1) I█████████████████ orway, turn
t█████████

2) If yo█████████ steps and choose either
passa███ ███ entrance to the dungeon,
turn to page 119.

Entering the cloud door could help you find out what has become of your father's castle and the fabulous treasure stored in its dungeon vaults or it could lead you to the dreaded lair of the Unknown Invader.

The choice is yours. Only you can choose the path that will return your kingdom to its old glory...or will lead you into the clutches of the evil wererat, Frang!

You Pick Your Own Path to Adventure!

An ENDLESS QUEST™ Book   #4

RETURN to BROOKMERE

BY ROSE ESTES

Cover Art by Larry Elmore
Interior Art by Timothy Truman

TSR Hobbies, Inc.

For my mother who taught me to reach.

Distributed to the book trade in the United States by Random House, Inc., and in Canada by Random House of Canada, Ltd.
Distributed in the United Kingdom by TSR (UK) Ltd.
Distributed to the toy and hobby trade by regional distributors.

TSR Hobbies, Inc.
POB 756
Lake Geneva, WI 53147

TSR Hobbies (UK) Ltd.
The Mill, Rathmore Road
Cambridge CB1 4AD
United Kingdom

ISBN 0-935696-93-8

9   8   7

First Printing — June 1982
Fifth Printing — March 1983

Printed in the United States of America
Library of Congress Catalog Card Number: 82-50452

Return to Brookmere is a
DUNGEONS & DRAGONS™ ENDLESS
QUEST™ Adventure book. Between the
covers of this book, you will find many
paths to fantasy adventure.

There are many possible choices and de-
cisions in this book; some simple, some
sensible, some foolhardy... and some
dangerous!

All the choices are up to you. You can read
the book many times with many different
results.

Remember, you choose the adventures in
the book. YOU are the adventure. We wish
you good adventuring and good luck!

In Return to Brookmere, you will be an elven fighter named Brion. As Brion, you are five feet tall and weigh 100 pounds. You have shoulder-length honey blonde hair, pointed ears, and brilliant gray-green eyes. Like all elves, you have elvensight allowing you to see objects up to 60 feet away in the dark by the heat they give off. Although elves are not as strong as humans, they are very clever and quick. Elves are able to speak the languages of orcs, goblins, hobgoblins, and gnolls as well as the "common" language of humans.

or your adventure, your father, King Cedrus, has given you a finely made suit of silvery chainmail that covers you from head to waist. Chain mail looks like a heavy knit silver sweater but it's woven from metal, not wool. Chainmail is light, flexible and will protect you in combat. You wear your chainmail under a purple wool tunic. Sturdy black leather breeches and tall black boots complete your outfit. You are armed with a sword and a dagger and carry a polished metal shield. A leather pouch filled with food and water is tied at your waist.

There is a heavy gold chain around your neck. At the end of the chain is a golden charm, worked in precious gems, in the shape of a dragon's head. The charm is the fabled amulet, the Mouth of Mimulus. With the help of this magical necklace, you will be able to speak with and understand any creature you meet on your adventure.

The dangers awaiting you will challenge your skills to the limit. Gather your wits about you. Take a firm hold on your sword. Turn the page and take the first step into... adventure!

You are leading a party of four elven fighters on a scouting mission to the ruins of your former home, Castle Brookmere.

Once this beautiful castle was filled with laughter and song. All that is gone now. Long ago, in the time of the Great Hunger, orcs, giants and other monsters swept down from the Far Frost Lands into Brookmere in search of food and treasure. They destroyed everything in their path including Castle Brookmere.

The outnumbered defenders of Brookmere were taken by surprise. They had no time to call on neighboring kingdoms for help. Although they fought valiantly, the elves had little hope of victory against the hordes of monsters. Your father, King Cedrus, sadly ordered his people to retreat to avoid their complete destruction.

Your family and friends fled Brookmere, saving only the few possessions they could carry on their backs. Your last memory of your beloved home is of foul monsters screaming insults at you from the captured castle's walls. Broken with grief, your father shook his fist at the ugly faces and vowed to return one day.

Now he has sent you on a quest with four elven fighters to discover what remains of his castle and the treasure hidden in the dungeon beneath it.

Your party stops at the edge of the forest that once ringed the castle and stares in disbelief. The only thing that still stands is the broken shell of a tower. All else is ruins. Scattered across the ground are enormous piles of boulders. The most noticeable feature on the ruined landscape is a wide black hole in the area of the castle that once housed the dungeon treasure vault.

With the aid of your friends, you push aside some of the rocks and follow a winding stairway down into the gaping hole. You are halfway down when the stairs and part of the walls collapse. You seem to fall forever and are knocked unconscious.

You awaken in silent darkness. Every bone in your body feels broken and your mouth is as dry as the desert. You wonder what has happened to your friends. Far above you, you can see a faint light and the rim of the hole. Below, you can make out the dim outline of a passageway leading into the dungeons.

1. If you decide to climb back up and search for your friends, turn to page 93.
2. If you decide to explore the passage-way, turn to page 36.
3. If you decide to sit quietly and think through your choices before you take any action, turn to page 29.

You realize too late you have made the wrong choice. Both hobgoblins fall on you, chuckling evilly. Although you fight boldly, you cannot win.

"I don't deserve this. I'm only an innocent bystander," shrieks Mim.

One of the hobgoblins rips Mim from your throat and puts it around its own grubby neck. Then the hobgoblin strolls down the corridor, humming off-key.

The End...
of this adventure. Go back to the beginning and choose again.

Once more dressed in your disguise, you enter the room and pretend to be a goblin. You say gruffly, "Quick! The walls in the orc's guard room have been broken down. Help them!"

All but two of the kobolds rush off. You laugh to yourself, knowing that Sissel will make short work of them.

The other two kobolds stand firmly in the middle of the room. They continue to stare stupidly at you. "We can't go unless Taurig tells us. You're not our leader. Taurig will be angry that the others left," says one of the kobolds.

Drawing your sword, you rush at them and kill both kobolds. Stepping over their bodies, you open the door on the right side of the room.

Fresh air blows against your face. You can smell the green scent of pine trees and meadows.

The amulet begins to sing in a deep booming voice, "Bene viburnum habitat esu, esqua, esqua, esqua!"

You know your mission is almost over. You can return to your father and tell him all you learned. Between your forces and Sissel's weasel army, you will destroy the enemy. Brookmere will be yours again!

The End...
of this adventure. Go back to the beginning and choose again.

You climb back to the entrance and sit in the sun, happy just to breathe the clean air. Once rested, you start toward home. You will tell your father your story. Perhaps one day another group will attempt to find out what is left of the castle. Until then, your family and friends must live in lonely exile with only memories of Castle Brookmere.

The End...
of this adventure. Go back to the beginning and choose again.

You take a torch from your pack and light it. Its sputtering flame dimly lights a dusty corridor.

"I was afraid you'd choose this path," grumbles a low voice.

Startled, you whirl around, hand on your sword, ready for combat.

The voice continues, "You know we're going to run into all sorts of monsters down here. Wouldn't you rather just turn around and go home?"

You look down at your chest in amazement. The amulet... the Mouth of Mimulus is talking. Your father told you that you could speak with monsters and animals with it, but he never told you the amulet, itself, could talk.

Though you feel silly talking to a necklace, you pick it up off your chest, look at it and say, "I promised my father I would discover what remained of Brookmere and whether our family could return."

Please turn to page 119.

"Well, here we are. On the path to doom, more than likely," groans Mim. "Well, at least clean me up. I've got dirt all over me from that fall we took."

"Can you talk all the time?" you ask. "Why didn't you say something before?"

"I talk when I have something to say, youngster. It's just that I wasn't worried until now. Well, never mind. Let's get going. By the way, please call me Mim. I detest being referred to as 'you'."

"Okay, Mim it is," you say and start down the passageway.

Walking is difficult as water drips from the walls and collects on the slippery stone floor. The green glow grows brighter.

A large boulder lies directly in front of you. A deep pool of water has collected at the base and is filled with small, blind cave fish and pale, large-eyed salamanders.

You avoid the pool and crawl around the boulder. The green glow is especially bright here after the dimness of the corridor.

You are in a small ruined room. At its far end is an archway dripping with a glowing green fungus. A bitter smell like rotting mushrooms fills your nostrils. Slowly, small pieces of the fungus break off and fall to the floor where they collect in a shimmering pool.

"I would advise you to be careful," says Mim. "This could be some variety of green slime. If it touches either of us, we're finished. Your father would never forgive me if I allowed us to be dissolved."

"I wouldn't like that much myself," you say. "I'm hoping this is simply a harmless fungus, like a mushroom."

"I certainly hope you're right," mutters Mim.

"Here goes!" you shout, and crossing your fingers for luck, you dash for the doorway. A glowing drop falls on you. You watch, too afraid even to breath, but nothing happens. You were right!! It was harmless.

You find yourself in another corridor, un-lit by the eerie green glow, but your torch sheds a little light. You hear moaning, snuf-fling and weeping sounds that sound like nothing you have ever heard before.

The corridor opens on one side into what once was a treasure room. Sitting on top of a pile of sparkling jewels in the center of the room is a young gnoll snuffling into a shabby golden tablecloth and talking to a bored salamander.

The gnoll looks like a hyena. It has greenish-gray skin, red-yellow hair and long sharp claws. It wears heavy gold chains, jeweled necklaces and a gem-studded crown. However, underneath its finery, its clothing is tattered and grimy.

The gnoll sits with its back to you and cries to the salamander. "They had no right to go off and leave me... I can't help it if I'm different than the rest...I don't like hurting and killing people. All those nasty orcs hanging around all the time gave me the creeps. I tried...really I did...but I couldn't learn to like tearing people limb from limb and all those other awful gnoll things.

"They always laughed at me because I was different. I've always liked pretty, shiny things.

"Golgal said to me, 'Nasnath, you'll never amount to anything. The only thing a real gnoll thinks about is destruction. You just stay here and play with your pretties. If and when you learn to act like a real gnoll, you can join us. Until then, stay here with the rats and salamanders.' Then they left me. I don't think that's fair, do you?" The salamander doesn't answer.

The corridor passes the room where the gnoll sits crying.

1. If you choose to go on without entering the room and fighting the gnoll, turn to page 71.
2. If you want to enter the room and fight the gnoll, turn to page 114.

They see you and attempt to rise but they are drunk and and you are sober. You quickly slay all three gnolls. Cleverly arranging the scene to look as though they had fought and killed each other in a drunken brawl, you hurry away down the corridor.

"Well, youngster, it's quite possible you will do well under my tutoring. I shall have to discuss a teaching position with your father when we return," says Mim.

Your earlier depression lifts and you rush along the corridor with a much lighter heart.

Ahead you see several oak doors with large locks. Strangely enough, there are no guards at the doors. One door has a huge iron key and one key ring dangling from the lock. Other keys hang on the ring. You wonder what is in the locked rooms. Taking the key in your hand, you unlock the heavy door. Creaking, it swings open. Holding your torch high, you look inside. Brilliant lights of rainbow colors flash in the torchlight.

"Look!" you shout excitedly. "All the gems in the world must be in this room. Where did they come from? This is ten times the amount of treasure my father owned."

"Very good! Excellent!" exclaims Mim. "We may yet be rewarded for our labors."

Quickly you seize the key ring and unlock the other rooms. Gleaming gold, shimmering silver and coldly flashing platinum are stacked to the ceilings. You race from room to room, shouting, "It's all here... all the treasure of Brookmere and much more. Father will be pleased beyond measure."

"I hate to interrupt," says Mim. "But where are the guards for these rooms? Why would treasure rooms such as these be left unguarded with a key hanging in the lock of the door?"

You step carefully into the corridor, sword and torch ready for action. There are no guards anywhere. The corridor, ceiling and floor look scrubbed clean. You pause, thinking that it is very unusual to see no dirt, no cobwebs, or moss in a dungeon, especially a dungeon inhabited by monsters.

You notice a strange, shimmering trail going down the corridor in the direction you were heading. Even as you watch the shimmer fades, then disappears.

"Maybe it's a giant snail," says Mim. "Once when I was in Hrothmer, we caught one and broiled it with butter and garlic. It was quite tasty and fed three platoons." You stare at the floor and wonder if you imagined the trail.

You shake your head to clear it. "Well, I don't know what it was but it's gone now. That's all I care about. We know the number of our enemies, their weaknesses and the location of the treasure. Let's not worry about who, what and why. Let's just get out of here. Once we tell my father all we've learned he can recapture the remains of his kingdom and rebuild it to surpass its former glory.

"Worrying about who, what and why is what has kept us alive until now," says Mim. "I suggest you keep asking yourself those questions." But you are pleased with yourself and do not answer. You stride down the corridor.

Entering a large room, you look around and see no guards. There are two wooden doors side by side leading out of the room, one to your left and the other to your right. You still wonder about the lack of guards by the entrance to the treasure room but shrug off Mim's concern.

Halfway across the room, you see something that makes your hair stand on end. A skeleton hangs about one foot off the floor against the far wall in front of the two doors. It still wears shreds of leather and metal armor. Still clutched in its bony hands are a sword and dagger. Even as you watch, some of the leather and bone slowly disappear. You notice the shimmery trail leads up to that spot and ends. Suddenly, the shimmering seems to ooze forward slowly. So does the skeleton.

You look more closely and see pieces of orcish armor all hanging in mid-air.

As you draw back in fear, your torch casts a slight reflection directly above the skeleton. You touch the reflection gingerly with your sword.

Immediately, you realize your mistake. It feels as though you have poked the sword into thick jam. Your sword seems to bend slightly and before your eyes an area 10 feet by 10 feet shimmers and wobbles like jelly. It is a gelatinous cube! A scavenger of the dungeons that dissolves anything foolish enough to be in its path.

Now that you know what you're looking at, it's dimensions are easy to see. It looks harmless but as the orcs found out, it's not. It glides toward you.

"As the wizard who created me would have said, "Bene atua lavernum!" says Mim.

"What does that mean?" you holler.

"Let's get out of here!" screams Mim.

1. If you decide to attack the cube with your sword, turn to page 129.
2. If you decide to use your torch against the cube, turn to page 133.

As you are drawn close to the awful mouth, you strike out with your sword. It cuts the giant's lip and strikes a huge front tooth as it is jarred from your hand.

"Ouch!" cries Furd, clasping both hands to its bleeding lip, and dropping you to the ground below. You lose your sword and are bruised and shaken. But at least you are alive.

"Run away! Run away!" screams Mim.

You don't need Mim to urge you. You run as fast as you can leaving Furd sitting on the ground holding its mouth and crying.

"Shut up, dummy," says Ool. "Or I'll give you something to cry about. Play more game."

You run like a deer down another tunnel you find behind some stones at the end of the room.

Please turn to page 57.

The slime is getting closer to your fingertips. You are starting to lose your nerve. You're afraid that it will reach your skin and eat you. You drop your cloak and it turns into a puddle of green slime as it hits the ground.

At that moment the gnoll rushes straight at you with drawn sword. Its blow throws you off balance and you fall into the puddle of green slime. It splashes on you, Mim and the gnoll. Even though you will perish, the gnoll will also die.

"Good grief, not me! Not meeeee..." shrieks Mim. Then all is silent.

The End...

of this adventure. Go back to the beginning and choose again.

You do not wish to rush off in the darkness. The shaky ground could collapse again and this time you might not come out alive. Hands on your aching head, you try to decide what to do.

"You might start by brushing the dirt out of my mouth," says a small voice. Are you hearing things? Who could be talking?

"Down here on your chest. Your amulet... the Mouth of Mimulus...the one with dirt in its mouth!" says the necklace.

Too startled to speak, you pick the heavy amulet up and hold it before your face.

"Blaff!" The jeweled mouth spits out a small piece of dirt. "Come on, come on. Don't just sit there like a lump. Brush me off!"

"I didn't know you could talk," you say, quickly brushing off the amulet.

"Ahh, much better. Now, youngster, since we seem to be fated to go through this adventure together, you better call me by my name, Mim. I detest being called Mouth or you. Now what are you going to do about this pickle you've gotten us into?"

"Well, I've not quite decided. I thought maybe I might go down and look around a bit."

"Unwise. Definitely unwise. What about your supplies and your friends."

"Well, I did think about going back and looking for them," you say.

"Make up your mind one way or the other. I strongly advise against going off alone into the dungeon."

"Okay, I won't go off alone. Let's go back and see where everyone is."

Slowly and with great difficulty, you climb the rock-strewn slope. You find your supplies and light a torch, but there is no trace of your friends. After searching carefully, you realize sadly that they are buried beneath the rock fall.

"Now what are we going to do?" asks Mim. "I seem to remember there is a secret path somewhere around here. Want to try it?"

1. If you want to go down and try to go on alone, turn to page 119.
2. If you want to try Mim's secret path, turn to page 37.

Holding Mim in front of you, you try to talk to the wolves.

"Do not attack," you say gently. "I am only a harmless elf. You are safe with me."

Mim groans loudly.

"Ahh, but you are not safe with us, little elf," growls Lars, the lead wolf. All three of the wolves leap on you. It's too late to draw your sword.

The wolves eat you. Now your father will never know what happened to you or his kingdom.

The End...

of this adventure. Go back to the beginning and choose again.

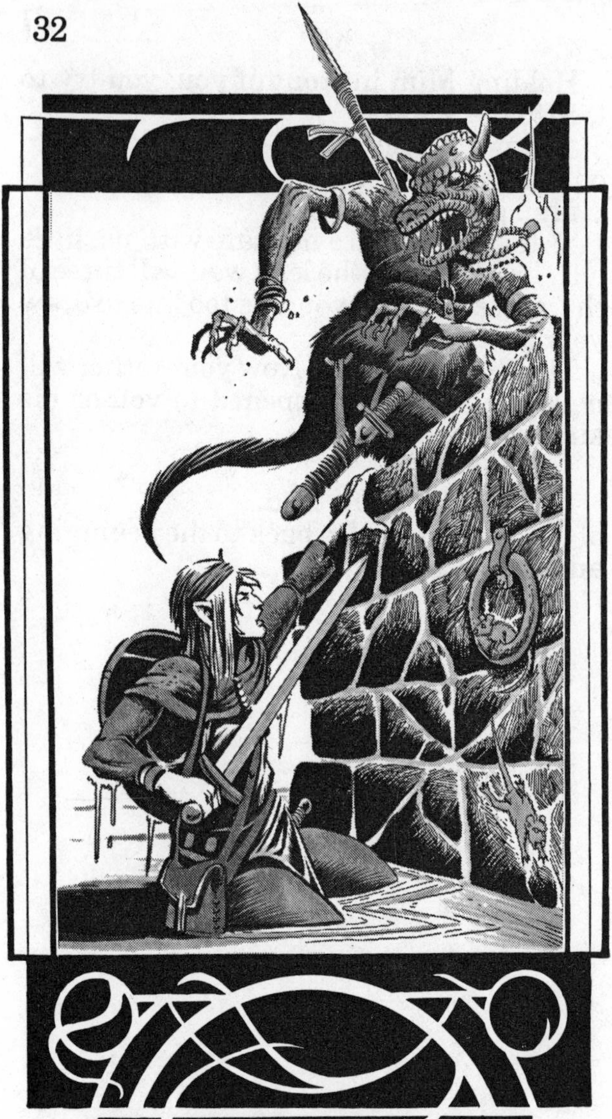

Despite the current, you manage to climb quietly out of the water. Clutching your sword firmly, you attack the kobold. It grasps its sword and leaps to its feet. The distance between you narrows. The kobold raises its sword for a massive blow. Just as the sword sweeps down, a powerful sneeze shakes the kobold. The sword flies out of its hand and lands in the water. The kobold lets out a terrible scream and dives in after it. The current seizes the kobold and sweeps it away into the darkness.

You sigh with relief and collapse next to the fire.

"It wasn't necessary to squeeze me quite that hard, Brion," says Mim. "A warning would have been quite sufficient."

"I'm sorry. I couldn't take the risk of the kobold hearing you."

"Stop lazing around and dry me off," snorts Mim.

After you dry and polish the amulet, you dry your own clothes in front of the fire. When you are warm and dry, you head through the doorway to the cave.

Please turn to page 55.

Even though it has a cold and is young, it is still a kobold and you know kobolds hate elves and would just as as soon kill elves then look at them. Not certain that you could win the battle, you allow the current to pull you away.

You are now unable to touch bottom and the current is much faster. Even with your elvensight, you can see nothing.

At last, cold and wet, you are swept into a pool of shallow water. You pull yourself up on some broken paving stones. You are in a cave dimly lit by glowing fungus. Too tired to explore further, you collapse on the rocks and fall into an exhausted sleep.

Memories of your mother singing to you as a child fill your mind and bring a smile to your lips. You strain to hear the words but they are unlike any your mother ever sang. When you finally make them out, your blood runs cold.

"Mash them, crash them, bash them. I will smash them. Crunch them, munch them, make them into lunch then! Bite their little fingers! Bite their little toes! Bite their little their ears off and don't forget their nose!"

You open your eyes and realize that the singing is coming from somewhere in the cave. It seems to be coming from behind a large boulder.

When you dare to look, you peer over the edge of the rock. You see a goblin sitting with its back to the river. It is a dirty yellow color. A spiked club and wooden shield lie by its side. The goblin must not have caught what it wanted to munch for lunch because it is nibbling some of the glowing fungus.

1. If you want to fight your way past the goblin to the tunnel, turn to page 51.
2. If you do not want to fight the goblin, turn to page 131.

You decide to take a quick look around before you go back to look for your friends. As you start to go down the stairs, your foot slips on a smooth rock. As you crash down on a pile of broken rock, you let out a loud cry. You roll to a stop, stunned by the fall. Shaking your head to clear it, you see three large, well-armed orcs standing by your side. Your cry has attracted their attention. Chuckling evilly, they surround you.

They pick you up, tie you securely, throw you over their shoulders, and walk off through the gloom.

The End...
of this adventure. Go back to the beginning and choose again.

"Well," you say, "father did say I would find you helpful. I suppose that I should rely on your decision. If you know a secret path, let's take it."

"What a clever elf you are!" says Mim. "Hmm... now, let me see. Which way is it? Oh, yes, over there to your right. Watch out for that boulder. Don't scratch my finish!"

Following Mim's directions, you pick your way down the rubble and ignoring a wide passageway with both left and right branches continue walking to your right. Soon, you lose all sense of direction.

"Are we almost there?" you ask.

"Soon, I think. Actually, I've never really taken this way before," answers Mim.

"What are you talking about? What do you mean you've never taken this path before? How will you know it when we get there?" you shout angrily.

"Trust me," says Mim.

"You've got five minutes to find the right path. Then I'm going to turn around and try to retrace my steps," you say.

Just then, off in the distance, you see a flickering light.

"Maybe that's it," you exclaim excitedly.

You hurry along the dark corridor. As you draw closer, you see that the light comes from a strange doorway set in the stone walls of the passageway. The darkness surrounds you yet the doorway glows with the brightness of a million lightning bugs. Thick white clouds puff and roll between the door frames. Stray wisps reach out toward you. Prickles of fear run up and down your spine.

"Is this it?" you ask Mim.

"I don't think so. Something doesn't feel right," says Mim.

"Listen, I'm getting worried," you say. "I think we're lost. We're looking for a secret path of some kind but you don't know what we're looking for. This is all we've seen so far. I think this is it!"

"If you go through that door, leave me here. I don't like this," says Mim.

1. If you go through the door and leave Mim behind, turn to page 52.
2. If you retrace your steps and choose either passage back at the entrance, turn to page 119.
3. If you want to listen to Mim and pass up the door and continue on, turn to page 64.

"I'm going to try to sneak up on them," you whisper to Mim.

"Fools rush in where angels fear to tread," warns Mim glumly.

You manage to creep up to within four paces of the orcs. They are deep in conversation and are not aware of you. While they talk, they share a cheap cigar that fills the corridor with smelly smoke.

"I don't care, Froiken. I still think we should have been allowed to go to the meeting. We're being punished because we fell asleep at our post last week," says one of the orcs.

"You're right, Farber. Sergeant Grunt was pretty angry or else we would never be stuck here in the boondocks. Still, this is a pretty important post. We guard one of the few tunnels that go outside. If any of those elves were brave enough to try to come back, this is the way they would come. Not that orcs would have any trouble with elves. We all know they are skinny little nothings who can't fight for beans."

Hearing this slur against elves, you become very angry. Skinny, little nothings, indeed!

"Can't fight for beans, can we? Take this!" you cry. Leaping forward, you attack Froiken. You land a lucky blow and the orc falls dead at your feet.

Farber turns, looks at you, then down at its slain friend. Its lips pull back in a snarl of hate showing its sharp yellow teeth. "You dare to attack an orc," it growls. "Come closer, little elf. I'm going to make hamburger out of you!"

"I can't watch," moans Mim.

You are in great danger. Gripping your sword, you step back and stand your ground. Your heart is pounding so loud, you are sure the orc can hear it.

With a last look at its fallen friend, the orc steps over the body, grinds its cigar out in the palm of its hand and attacks.

The fight is short and fierce. Judging that you are no match for it, the orc fights carelessly. You lunge at the orc and stab it in the chest with your sword. The fatally wounded orc mutters, "Who would have thought I could have been beaten by an elf."

You have not escaped injury. Your arm is slashed in several places and bleeds heavily. Taking a clean cloth and medicine from your pouch, you bind your wounds.

"May I congratulate you," Mim exclaims. "Your father would be so proud of you. I suggest that you prop the dead orcs up so they appear to be sleeping at their posts again."

You agree with Mim and, overcoming your dislike for orcs, dead or alive, arrange them as suggested.

You hurry down the corridor looking from side to side for danger. The passage winds on. It seems to be in much better condition than the rooms you have travelled through up until now.

Torches are stuck in metal holders and spaced evenly on the walls. You worry about meeting monsters in the lighted corridor, but meet no one. All the rooms off the corridor look empty.

You open one door and discover a treasure storeroom. In it you see many of the fine works of art that belonged to your father. But there are also treasures you don't recognize.

"Oh, marvelous, they didn't destroy the Flabbermott. It was always one of my favorites. Such colors, such composition... divine!" sighs Mim.

You look around, but all you can see is a painting of an old elf wearing royal robes and a crown. "Oh, him. That's my grandfather. He was nice. I remember him well."

"No, not your grandfather. I was speaking of the glorious Flabbermott he's wearing."

Your attention is drawn to the painting and you notice that an amulet hangs from your grandfather's neck.

"He never went anywhere without it. He always said the Flabbermott was his trusted friend and advisor. Maybe you should do the same."

"I never knew what happened to my grandfather. Do you?"

"I believe he and the Flabbermott disappeared in the campaign of '76 against the orc hordes," says Mim knowingly.

"Obviously, the Flabbermott didn't help my grandfather much. If all you can do is hang around someone's neck and talk, that's not much help, is it?"

"My dear young man, I'm afraid your tender age betrays your lack of knowledge. Amulets are far more than just amusing talking toys. I have at my command some valuable spells including a powerful sleep spell that just might serve us well. Although, I pray we have no use for them."

"What? You've had magic spells all this time and never used them. You let me take all these risks when you could have done something easy and magical? How could you do that? Show me a spell right now!" you demand.

"All in its proper time," says Mim. "Come along, now. We've got work to do."

"I'm telling you now, faithful amulet of my father, you're part of this adventure even though I didn't invite you along. So, if we get in another tight spot, I don't want talk, I want action," you tell Mim sternly.

"When I was your age, I respected my elders," sputters Mim.

Ignoring this, you check out the rest of the room. The monsters have added the treasure they took from other kingdoms. You take nothing but again make note of the location.

You open another door and find a room full of weapons. They stand upright in wooden racks, row upon gleaming row. You are tempted to add another more dangerous weapon to your own small sword and dagger. However, since each rack of weapons is clearly labeled with an orcish name, you decide that it would be suspicious if one were missing.

Farther on, you find rooms used as orc barracks. Wooden bunk beds are built three high against the walls. The room is empty and smells like a stable. The beds are unmade and armor and pieces of dirty orc underwear litter the floor. Pictures of female orc beauties are on the walls. A wooden table in the middle of the room is covered with torn cards and a set of dice made from real bones.

You leave the room quickly. Ahead of you, the tunnel divides. As you try to decide which way to go, you hear a loud noise. Peeking carefully around the corner, you see a young goblin and a sniffling kobold standing about 20 paces away. They are both yelling at the top of their lungs at a group of three adult goblins and two kobolds. With all the shouting, you can't make out what they're saying.

One of the adult goblins thunders, "Shut up!"

Pointing a knobby-nailed finger at the small excited goblin it says, "Now, one at a time. Tell us what this is all about." Both creatures start to speak at the same time.

An angry goblin yells, "Be Quiet!" Taking the young goblin by its ear, it pulls it forward. "Speak up, Karsh, and this had better be good. We're late for the meeting because of you."

Karsh tries to pull away from the painful tug on its ear but does not succeed. Pointing its gnarled finger at Karsh's face, the adult goblin growls, "Now, talk and be quick about it!"

"Yes sir. Yes sir," says Karsh, standing on tiptoe trying to keep its ear connected to its head.

"We both saw a stranger...an elf. I saw it first," says Karsh.

"No," exclaims the young kobold, "I saw the elf first and beat it up."

"No, you didn't," says Karsh.

"I did. I saw the elf first and punched it hard. Then, the elf threw a magic spell that froze me. It turned invisible and disappeared or I would have killed it for sure."

"No, you didn't," hollers the young kobold.

"Be quiet," yell all the adults and the youngsters shut up.

The big goblin shakes Karsh by its ear until it hollers.

The adult goblin roars, "Where and when did this happen?"

Karsh begins to sniffle, "In the water caves, I saw it there a little while ago."

The large goblin gives Karsh a final shake, then drops him.

Karsh rubs its ear, now a bright orange, and starts to cry quietly. The adult monsters turn toward the young kobold who tries to appear braver than Karsh, but is truly frightened by the angry adults. It places both hands over its ears and backs up to the wall. "I really did hit the elf," the young kobold mumbles.

"We don't care about that," snarls an adult kobold. "Just tell us where you were and if the elf was armed."

The young kobold removes its hands from its ears and tries to look a little braver.

"It was in the water caves, just a little while ago and the elf only has an old sword. I could have beaten it, if I'd wanted to," brags the young kobold.

"Think they saw something?" asks one goblin.

"You know how kids are," replies a kobold. "Probably not."

"Oh yeah? Well, maybe that's how a kobold kid is, but if a goblin kid says it saw someone, it saw someone. I say we split up and check the water caves for the invader. If there really is an elf in the dungeons, we'll make short work of it."

After arguing about which group should go where, the adults rush off toward the water caves to look for you.

The two young monsters are left in the corridor, glaring fiercely at each other.

"What utter and complete monsters those kids were," says Mim.

"Don't worry about them. Think about us! Which way should we go?"

Mim is silent.

"Don't clam up on me. Please, I need your advice. Which way should we head?" You give Mim a hard shake but it doesn't speak.

"Terrific!" you say, dropping Mim in disgust on your chest.

Now you must make the choice on your own.

1. If you choose to go down the left corridor, turn to page 57.
2. If you choose to try the right corridor, turn to page 55.

You gather all your strength and draw your sword. Screaming a battle cry, you throw yourself at the goblin.

Mim screams loudly, "Lardaloohoo!"

The goblin is so startled that it drops the piece of fungus it is nibbling and runs out the door. Looking back over its shoulder, it shouts, "You better watch out. I'll be back with my big brother." It disappears down the corridor.

"Well done. First rate," praises Mim. "But just in case that beastly little brat meant what it said, let's keep going. I, for one, have no desire to meet its big brother."

You don't wish to enter the cold water again. You creep into the corridor hoping that a new tunnel will appear, offering you another choice in case the young goblin does come back with its big brother.

Please turn to page 57.

"Listen, Mim, Father gave you to me to be helpful. So far, you haven't been much help. Now this door looks promising. It's all dark and scary in the passageway. Unless you can think of a good reason I shouldn't go through it, I'm going!" you say firmly.

"I can't give you any reason why not. It just doesn't feel right to me," says Mim.

"Just give me an answer. What do you think is on the other side?" you ask.

"Nothing," says Mim.

"That does it," you say. "Are you coming with me?"

"If you insist on this, please take me off and put me somewhere safe." You take the amulet off and hang it on a hook by the door.

"Goodbye," says Mim.

"Goodbye," you say. Grasping the shimmering doorway, you place your head and upper half of your body in the misty clouds and try to see what lies ahead.

For a minute, nothing happens, then slowly the lower part of your body begins to glow and shimmer with an unearthly light.

"I don't think I like the looks of this," says Mim.

The glow fades. The outline of your body can still be seen but it starts to smudge and blur. Soon, all that is left is white, billowing smoke moving gently in the quiet corridor, then drifting through the door and becoming part of the larger cloud mass.

"Now, I remember!" says Mim. "It's a Door of Nothingness.

"Anyone who passes through it turns to nothing. Poor Brion. No one can fault me. I hope King Cedrus will see it that way. He'll probably be so angry he'll melt me down into a doorstop.

"Well, there are worse things than hanging here. One must learn to make the best of things. My gems probably look quite charming in this soft light."

The End...

of this adventure. Go back to the beginning and choose again.

This corridor is well lighted and seems to be heavily travelled. Fortunately, the corridor frequently twists and turns. You hear the heavy tramp of boots and duck into an empty room just as a patrol of armed orcs and goblins come around a corner and march past. They are marching away from you. You pick up scattered bits of conversation and conclude that they are all going to a meeting.

After they pass, you sneak back into the corridor and continue. Before you know it, you are in a large room where a battle has recently taken place. You see two heavily armed hobgoblins at either end of the room. You quickly hide behind a large chest.

Behind you is a cloakroom holding many tattered and rumpled goblin and hobgoblin cloaks and helmets. Deciding to use them as a disguise, you slip a goblin cloak on and put a helmet on your head. You carefully tuck your blonde hair inside the hood of your cloak. The wall on the far side of the room shows great destruction. Most of the stonework has fallen into the room. Large boulders lie scattered about the floor and the earthern wall is braced with a crisscross of metal plates held in place with massive wooden beams.

At first you think the destruction was caused during the battle for Brookmere, then you realize from the heavy armor they are wearing and the watchful expressions on the faces of the hobgoblins that something has recently broken into the corridor from the outside.

1. If you choose to leap out from behind the chest and attack the hobgoblins, turn to page 99.
2. If you choose to try to sneak across to the corridor on the opposite wall, turn to page 150.

You creep carefully down the corridor. A loud murmuring sound makes you move even more slowly. A room opens on your right. Inside, lit by flickering torches, you see a large gathering of adult gnolls. All are dressed in full battle armor and carry shields, battle axes, swords, clubs, daggers and other nasty weapons.

There is a large pile of rubble in the center of the room and a large gnoll stands on top of it. Its leather armor is decorated with rib bones. A necklace of finger bones hangs around its neck and small skulls hang from its belt. Its yellow eyes gleam in the firelight.

"Listen!" it growls. "It's not that I really want to join goblins, orcs and others, but we have to."

"Oh yeah, Belcher? Who says?" cries a voice from the crowd. "When do gnolls have to do anything they don't want to."

"Since Frang says so, that's since when," replies Belcher, the gnoll leader. "I don't like it either, but I'm not about to tell Frang. Are you?"

There is only silence from the crowd.

58

"That wererat is just too evil and too powerful for us. If we were dumb enough to say no, we'd be as good as dead. Those who were left would still have to deal with Frang. Anyway, I, Belcher, have decided. If you're too stupid to understand, you can always fight me." It leans forward glaring at its troops. Once again, there is only silence.

"Let's not waste time arguing. If we join Frang, there's going to be enough killing for everyone. When it's all over, this dungeon will still be big enough for all of us. What do you say?"

The gnolls start to shout all together, "Break! Rip! Tear! Kill!" until the room echoes with their hideous cries.

Before the gnolls discover you, you sneak past the room and rush down the corridor. You are moving so fast that before you can stop you run straight into an open room.

An armed gnoll is sitting with its back to you in the middle of the room. It is gnawing on a bone and throwing dice against the far wall.

1. If you want to try to sneak past the gnoll and go into the corridor on the far side of the room, turn to page 55.
2. If you want to attack the gnoll, turn to page 62.

You advance quietly. When you are almost within striking range, your toe strikes a pebble that clatters across the floor. The gnoll looks up from its game and drops the bone and dice. It lets out a roar and starts after you. You speed off down the corridor. The gnoll is about ten paces behind you. But you are faster and lighter and it is loaded down with armor.

The corridor is short and as you sprint around a bend, you find yourself in another small cave covered in glowing green fungus. It hangs over the ceiling and walls and drips from the doorway. Since it looks the same, you make the mistake of assuming it is harmless, edible fungus. As you speed through the doorway, a piece of it falls on your cloak. Instead of bouncing off harmlessly, it hisses and bubbles and burns through the fabric. It's green slime!

"Oh, no!" cries Mim. "You've made a terrible mistake. Don't let it touch us or it will dissolve your flesh and my beautiful gems."

You don't need Mim to tell you that you are in a fix. Thinking fast, you realize you have two choices, neither of them appeals to you.

Quickly you take off your cloak making sure that it doesn't touch your body and hold it far away from you. You draw your sword and turn. The gnoll enters the room and spotting you gives a shrill cry of triumph.

The cloak dangles from your trembling fingers. The slime has dissolved half of the cloak, hissing and bubbling as it moves.

The gnoll slides to a halt five paces from you.

"Got you now, elfie. You can't win. Just save us both some trouble and surrender," chuckles the gnoll evilly.

1. If you want to drop the cloak and fight the gnoll, turn to page 28.
2. If you want to try to fool the gnoll and let it think you are surrendering, turn to page 66.

"I still don't see why we can't go through the door. It looks interesting to me."

"Interesting, yes. Safe, no," answers Mim. "Personally, I'd rather be safe than sorry."

"I guess you're right. I can't take any chances when the whole kingdom depends on me. We'll go on, but I hope something happens soon. I'm getting discouraged."

"Something will happen. I'm positive of it," says Mim firmly. "Let's go."

You continue through the dark, winding corridors. Even though you see signs that monsters have passed through there, you do not meet any.

Finally, the corridor comes to an end. You are in a dead end, a wall of brick from floor to ceiling blocks your way. There are no side corridors. There seems to be no way to continue.

1. If you want to turn around and retrace your steps back to one of the two passages at the entrance, turn to page 119.
2. If you decide that you want to check out the cloud door, turn to page 52.
3. If you want to sit down and try to figure out why the corridor ended in a dead end, turn to page 75.

Looking sad and frightened, you take a step toward the gnoll. Quickly, you whirl your cloak upward, flinging it directly at the gnoll's head. It wraps itself around the monster's head, neck, and shoulders in hissing folds. The gnoll drops its sword and staggers around the room crashing into slime-covered walls. Green slime means certain death. You do not stop to watch, but rush out of the room and down the corridor.

"Oh," shudders Mim. "That was awful. Where did you learn that trick?"

"Be quiet, Mim!" you hiss angrily. "Don't be such a coward. I did what I had to do. Be glad you weren't dissolved or killed by the gnoll."

Mim is silent.

Please turn to page 55.

Removing the goblin cloak, you advance with drawn sword. You still wear the horned goblin helmet on your head.

Kobolds are shorter and less powerful than elves. You also have the advantage of surprise.

Before the kobolds can recover and attack, you slay all of them.

You are wounded in several places but not seriously.

"I wish you'd pay more attention to my warnings. I really want to help you," says Mim.

Opening the door on the left, you hurry from the room.

You run along the corridor, pleased that you have done what you set out to do. An exit cannot be too far away. You see a door on your right.

Please turn to page 141.

"Slow down. All this bouncing might damage me," yells Mim as it flops about on your chest.

Turning a bend in the corridor, you come on a hill giant sitting on a boulder. You can't stop running. Your speed carries you forward until you crash headlong into its legs. At the last moment, it sees you but is too surprised to react.

Your breath is knocked out of you. Stunned, you fall to the ground. Your head spins and you see four giants.

"Hey!" rumbles the giant. "That hurt." It picks you up by your tunic and peers closely at you. It pokes you with a grubby finger and swings you lazily back and forth. Now, you see eight giants.

"It's an elf! What's an elf doing here? Frang hates elves. Speak, elfie!"

Your head is spinning. You know you can't last long.

1. If you want to take your chances and attack the giant, turn to page 137.
2. If you want to try to talk the giant into letting you go, turn to page 139.

Mim casts the sleep spell at the larger of the two hobgoblins. It drops like a lead weight to the floor. Surprised and confused, its partner rushes over to it and begins to shake it saying, "Taurig, what's the matter? Get up!"

Without a moment's pause, you attack from the rear. You slice the hobgoblin across the back of its knees, the only unarmored part of its body.

Shrieking, the hobgoblin turns and draws its sword. Horribly wounded, it is still a dangerous enemy.

You circle warily. The hobgoblin uses all its cunning and strength, but your blows wear it down. At last, you deliver the killing blow. Weak with relief, you sag against the wall.

"Excellent," crows Mim. "That last parry and thrust was classic! As my old fencing master Baron de Rapier would have said..."

"Listen, I'm sorry but I'm too tired to listen to your tales now. You never talk when I need you," you snap tiredly.

"Well," huffs Mim, "I won't waste my breath then," and retreats into sulky silence.

As you leave the room, you pass a row of goblin and hobgoblin cloaks hanging on pegs. Slipping a goblin cloak and helmet off a peg, you put them on to wear as a disguise. Hurrying out of the room, you dash into the corridor.

Please turn to page 150.

Enormous boulders, dirt, and fallen timbers are scattered about the passageway blocking your path. The tunnel must have been this way since your kingdom fell. You push your way through rubble.

You accidentally bump into a beam and dirt trickles down from the ceiling. From time to time, you hear a loud rumble and booming sound in the tunnel.

"I think we should be very careful," says Mim. "This area looks most unsafe."

"Of course, I'm going to be careful," you whisper angrily. "You aren't much help, you know."

Mim retreats into moody silence. Moving slowly and silently, you turn a corner. Hearing voices nearby, you sneak up to the next turn in the corridor and peer carefully around.

You see two ugly, human-like creatures standing about 10 feet tall. Hair grows down over their low foreheads and hangs in their eyes. They are covered with mangy animal skins. Coarse hair grows all over their slouched bodies.

"What are they?" you ask Mim.

"Hill giants," Mim answers. "Try to avoid them. They aren't too bright and they could squash us without even trying."

At the far end of the long and narrow room are a number of tall, thin stones.

"Har! Har! Har!" laughs the first giant. "Missed that one, Furd. Didn't even come close."

"You bump Furd. That why Furd miss," accuses Furd, the second giant.

"That how Ool play. Set up stones for new game," orders Ool.

"Why Furd always do it," whines Furd.

"You always loser, that's why. Har! Har! Har!" snorts Ool.

Furd turns around and starts to pick up the stones for a new game. It picks up the rock you are hiding behind. You're seen! There's nowhere to escape!

Furd picks you up by your tunic and holds you high in the air.

"Hey, Ool, look at what Furd find," Furd mutters.

You kick your feet but the giant just shakes its head and laughs.

"Kind of cute. What is it, Ool?" asks Furd.

"Is elf, dummy. Give to me. Need food. Only had a handful of rats today," demands Ool.

"No, mine. Furd find it. Furd keep it," says Furd clutching you in its enormous hand.

"Don't care," says Ool. "Got dried lizards to eat. You eat it. Play more game. Ool like game. Har! Har! Har!"

Furd holds you close to its beady eyes and says, "Do it taste good?"

1. If you choose to wait until you are about to be eaten and then attack the giant, turn to page 27.
2. If you want to use your wits and try to trick the giant, turn to page 94.

You sit on the floor and stare at the wall in front of you.

"Who would build a dead end in a dungeon?" you ask Mim.

"I don't understand this," says Mim. "I know we've chosen correctly. I feel all tingly as though something wondrous is about to happen."

You stand up and run your hands over the walls looking for a secret door. You find nothing.

You start to knock on the walls looking for a hollow place. But the walls are solid stone and you find nothing.

"Let me see. Oh, do let me help! I can't bear to just hang around your neck helplessly," cries Mim.

"Mim, you can talk but you can't see. How can you help me?" you reply.

"Don't be so picky. In my own way, I 'see' better than you. Hold me up, please," orders Mim.

"Well, I'm not finding anything. Maybe you can locate something I can't," you admit.

Holding Mim at head height, you pass it over the surrounding walls and ceiling. At first nothing happens. You cover almost the entire end of the passageway. Sudderl- brilliant beams of red and blue flash out o the wall and strike Mim.

"Stop! That tickles!" shrieks Mim. A tin- gling feeling passes through the golden necklace and down your fingertips, numb- ing your entire hand. Shocked by the unex- pected feeling, your fingers open and Mim tumbles to the ground.

"Take some care, you clumsy elf. You dropped me!" exclaims Mim.

You bend over and try to find the amulet in the dim light cast by your torch. A strong draft of cold air drifts over you and blows your torch out. You are in total darkness.

"Who goes there?" challenges a ghostly voice. "Who dares to enter this chamber un- invited? Stand and identify yourselves."

Grasping the amulet, you rise. The wall has disappeared and you are now standing at the edge of a darkened doorway.

"Can it be? Is that you, Mazahs?" questions Mim eagerly.

"You dare to mention the name of Mazahs!" thunders the voice, as purple and red streaks of lightning shoot forth menacingly.

"Listen, Mazahs, stop the cheap tricks. I'm not afraid of you," roars Mim in a loud, frightening voice. Emerald green sparks fly through the air and thunder booms.

"Mimulus? Is that you?" asks the voice.

"Yes, it's me, you ninny. Why is it so dark in here? Let's have some light!" commands Mim.

"Mimulus, you don't have to yell. I'm only doing my job," says Mazahs timidly.

"You couldn't balance a brick on your nose much less do your job!" hollers Mim.

"Oh yeah? Just watch!" yells Mazahs. Before your startled eyes, a glow of light fills the air. A brick appears out of the gloom and rises in the air. It floats without support in the stale dungeon air.

"What does that prove, you quack?" says Mim. "You could be holding it in your hands. Materialize, you fake!"

"Quack! Fake! Who are you to call me a fake. At least I have a body. All you are is a dragon's head with a big mouth. I'll show you who's a fake," replies Mazahs.

Slowly out of the gloom, a shape forms. You cannot clearly make out features but you can see what seems to be a head, body and legs. In fact, there are more than the usual number of legs and the body seems strangely shaped.

"Look!" says Mazahs. Balancing the brick on its nose, it floats back and forth in the air.

"I applaud you, Mazahs," says Mim. "But why are you still here? Your mission should have been over long ago."

"I thought it would too," says Mazahs sadly. "I want to leave but I have been commanded to stay here until my Master returns. I am bound here until he returns and sets me free."

"Where is he?" asks Mim.

"Oh, he's still here. . .it's his mind that's missing," replies Mazahs.

"I think we need an explanation," says Mim.

"Come over here. I'll show you," says Mazahs as it drifts slowly away.

"Don't just stand there. Follow him!" orders Mim sharply.

You quickly move to follow the shadowy form of Mazahs.

It floats across a wide distance filled with small and large objects. A blue glowing light hovers above Mazahs and provides some light for your path. In the gloom, you bump into small objects that hurt your ankles and large objects that knock the breath out of you.

Holding your hands before you, you manage to avoid any serious accidents.

"Oh, do be careful." says Mazahs. "If you break anything, I'll have to pay for it before I'm allowed to leave."

"Be a good chap then and light our way," says Mim.

"I can't turn on the lights, Orobius wouldn't like it. You remember how cheap he is, Mim!" says Mazahs.

Suddenly Mazahs says, "You see. There he is," and points into the darkness ahead.

Following Mazahs at a rapid pace, you pass under a carved white marble arch engraved with words from some forgotten language. The thick dust on the floor rises in little puffs at your every step. There is a strange feeling all around you and you are reluctant to move farther. Mim urges you on saying, "Hurry up! Do hurry! It's the Master! It's Orobius!"

You see a white marble throne. Its back is to you as you approach. The strange feeling grows heavier. You drag your feet in the dust and approach even more slowly.

Before the throne stands a table of white marble. On top of the table is a single piece of clear crystal. It rises in a tall triangle at least three feet tall balancing on a tiny, sharp point. At the base of the crystal is a mixture of colors ... red, blue, gold, green. Radiating out from the delicate base, the colors ebb and flow ever mixing, changing and separating. All the colors of the rainbow are in the crystal. As the colors rise and separate into thin threads of brilliant gem colors, you notice that the upper part of the crystal contains a picture painted by the colors.

"You see. He's been sitting there like that staring at that picture since the big battle. His mind is still out there somewhere. I can't leave until he comes back and frees me," says Mazahs.

You cannot see who or what is sitting in the chair. All of your attention is held by the most amazing sight.

Curiosity overcomes fear. Ignoring all else, you rush to the crystal. Looking into it you see... yourself as a young child carried in your mother's arms as your family flees Brookmere. The colors painting the scene do not move. They hold forever the scene of Brookmere's defeat. You can see the castle being destroyed by a vast army of monsters who appear to be following on your very footsteps. The picture reminds you of tales of the miraculous escape from Brookmere... tales of how escape was made when no escape seemed possible. Some unknown force had stopped the monsters.

The monsters seemed frozen in their tracks until the last of your people escaped. Before you is the picture of the escape. You stare at the crystal drinking in the details. Gradually, you return to reality and turn excitedly to Mazahs who stands behind you.

"Do you know what this is?" you say. Then the words seems to die on your lips. Seated before you on the white marble throne is Orobius, the Master Illusionist of Brookmere.

"Be careful. Don't touch him," says mazahs. "If you awaken him, he'll lose the picture and be very angry with me."

"Don't worry," you say gently. Sinking to your knees, you sit on the dusty floor and stare in wonder at Orobius.

You look at the dust-covered figure before you. "He won't wake up," you say sadly.

"How do you know? What do you mean?" asks Mazahs.

"He's dead," says Mim softly.

"Dead, how can he be dead? All these years I've stayed by his side. 'Don't leave until I awaken,' he commanded. There was no way I could twist that command. I could have taken him with me, gone home and still obeyed the command. I was afraid if I left, he'd wake up and extend my sentence. Now you tell me he's dead. How could this happen?" asks Mazahs.

"I'm sure you deserve much praise," says Mim. "His death had nothing to do with you, Mazahs, my friend. You see the scene in the crystal? That was his last and greatest illusion...more than he could survive. Through his great powers he was able to summon up this scene in the crystal. He projected his mind and halted the advance of the monsters until those of Brookmere who remained alive could escape. After that, his powers were so drained that he was unable to return to his body and he died.

Kneeling on the dusty floor, you stare up at the remains of Orobius.

A thin golden circlet rests on his flowing mane of silvery hair. He wears a purple robe heavily embroidered with golden magical signs. His features are noble even in death. His hands rest palm down on the table.

"Then, I'm free!" says Mazahs. Before your eyes you see the dusty outline of its body slide to the floor like a cast-off robe. Dust swirls as Mazahs glides about the room laughing. Its sounds of joy whirl about your ears in a rush of damp dungeon air.

You hear a strange noise like a spinning top that has run down and is starting to topple over. You look up through the clouds of dust and see the crystal revolving in wide, slow circles starting to fall.

As though caught in slow motion, you reach out to try and catch it. It falls striking the white marble table. Many long jagged cracks appear and a hissing sound is heard. The picture begins to blur and fade and the colored streams ooze out of the cracks. The threads rise, intertwine and drift upward into the gloom. The crystal lies on the table broken and lifeless.

Behind you there is a sound like sand softly blowing on the beach. You turn and see that the remains of Orobius are falling to dust before your eyes. Soon, nothing is left of the Master Illusionist but the gold circlet, some heavy gold chains, and the purple robe.

Once again the joyous laughter surrounds you. Great clouds of dust rise. Then trailing its eerie wail, the shadowy form disappears from sight.

"Where did Mazahs go? What was it?" you ask Mim.

"Mazahs is an invisible stalker. Orobius captured it and used it for protection when he was 'seeing' one of his illusions. Invisible stalkers are known for their ability to bend the words of a command to fit their own needs. Orobius was too clever for Mazahs. He left it no loopholes. The poor creature spent all these years keeping watch over a dead man. Now that we have freed Mazahs of its command, I imagine it is back in its own world. There is nothing else here for us."

You don't need the amulet's urging to leave this place of sadness. Following the amulet's directions, you hurry across the dusty floor and soon come to a raised block of white marble standing between four white marble pillars.

"Yes, this is it," says Mim.

"This is what?" you ask.

"This is a Portal of Transport," answers Mim. "If we stand on the platform, we can transport ourselves anywhere we wish."

1. If you choose to go home and ask for more help, turn to page 12.
2. If you want to go back to the entrance and choose one of the two tunnels, turn to page 119.
3. If you want to transport closer to the center of the dungeon, step into the Portal and turn to page 106.

You start the difficult climb to the entrance. Large boulders, dirt, and heavy wooden beams move beneath your feet. Groaning noises make you fear the whole tunnel might crash down on your head at any moment.

Searching carefully, you find your torch and sword. There is no sign of any of your friends. You are alone, you feel that going on alone is dangerous but your father has trusted you with this most important quest. You know you can't let him down.

1. If you want to give up and return to the surface, turn to page 12.
2. If you want to explore the dungeon, turn to page 14.

You say, "Don't eat me, Furd. I'm just a skinny elf. Besides, I can teach you how to beat Ool at the game."

"You try to trick Furd?" says Furd.

"No, it's not a trick. It's not fair that Ool wins all the time. You play better than he does. I saw Ool bump you so you'd lose. If you put me down, I'll help you win."

"Why are you whispering with it?" shouts Ool.

"Not talking about anything, Ool," says Furd. "Mine... Furd find it... Furd can talk to it if Furd want."

Then Furd whispers to you suspiciously, "You help Furd win?"

"Yes, I'll run down and stand in front of the stones and make a lot of noise to attract attention. You aim your boulder at me. Then at the last minute, I'll jump aside. Your boulder will knock down the stones and you'll win. If you miss, I'll knock the stones over and you'll still win. Okay?"

"Hey, okay," says Furd. "Good idea. Furd like it. I win. Then Ool have to set up stones. Har! Har! Har!"

Furd wrinkles its forehead and frowns at you. "How I know you won't trick Furd?" it says.

"I wouldn't do that," you say. "You're too smart for me. After all, you caught me, didn't you?"

Furd scrunches its face up in a terrible smile. "You right. Furd too smart. Har! Har! Har!"

Furd walks down to the end of the room and puts you in front of the stones. It picks up a boulder and gets ready to throw.

"Hey, Furd," says Ool. "Not your turn. Ool's turn."

"No, I go now!" howls Furd. "I go first. You not want Furd to win game."

Furd takes its club and strikes Ool on the head. Ool staggers but picks up its own club and returns Furd's blow.

In the midst of the fight, you slip away.

Hearing Ool and Furd still arguing, you dash into the corridor. You hurry on your way without looking back at the fighting giants.

"Well, kiddo, you handled that quite well," says Mim. "I couldn't have done better myself."

"Listen, you fancy piece of talking metal. You're not much help to me. When I need to know something, you won't talk to me. But when I don't need help, you won't shut up. I should just throw you away!" Reaching up, you grab the heavy chain that holds Mim.

"Think of what your father would say if you do that," screams Mim.

You think for a minute then snatching a small piece of cloth from your pouch, you stuff it in Mim's mouth.

"Okay, I might have to keep you but I don't have to listen to you!"

"Mpff, glrg," mumbles Mim.

Pleased with yourself, you continue on your way.

A dark room opens off the corridor to your left. Your elvensight shows you that no one is in the room. It is a supply room used by the monsters. You find an old sword, some dried fruit, a wedge of cheese, and a jug of water. After eating your fill, you sink down on a pile of furs and snuggle into them. Pulling them up over your head, you fall deeply asleep.

Hours later, you awaken feeling renewed. Rummaging through the supplies, you find a goblin cloak and a helmet among the stores. Thinking that they might make a good disguise, you slip them on. To complete the disguise, you tuck your blonde hair down inside the hood of the goblin cloak. You put some more food in the pouch and refill your water flask. Grasping your sword, you step into the corridor.

There is a light at the end of the corridor. Creeping quietly to the archway, you peek around. What you see is so frightening that you almost want to go back and take your chances with the giants. You see a bugbear! You groan to yourself. A bugbear is a terrifying and sneaky opponent. As you stare, you see that it is carefully sharpening several swords and spears. It seems to be concentrating on its work, but suddenly says, "Heard you coming through the darkness. Good ears, you know."

The bugbear's evil, red eyes stare at you. "Come out. I have special sight, too. So, the dark won't help you. Don't bother to run because I can run faster than you."

1. If you want to try to fight the bugbear, turn to page 102.
2. If you want to pretend you are following the bugbear's instructions and try to fool it, turn to page 100.

Giving a blood curdling yell, you leap out from behind the boulder. Instead of being frightened, the two hobgoblins advance toward you. You realize that this was not a wise choice.

1. If you want to try to fight both hobgoblins, turn to page 9.
2. If you want to try to have Mim cast its sleep spell at one hobgoblin and then try to fight the other, turn to page 69.
3. If you want to retreat, turn to page 12.

You decide to take the risk. You enter the room as though following the bugbear's orders. Suddenly you speed up and run as fast as you can into the bugbear. You know you can't hurt it, but you do succeed in knocking it off balance. By the time the bugbear regains its balance, you are speeding down the corridor to the right and are gone.

Please turn to page 68.

With drawn sword, you advance on the bugbear. It circles you, swinging a battleaxe. If the battleaxe hits you, you are dead. Pretending not to understand the danger you are in, you move closer and closer to the whistling axe. The bugbear thinks it has met a stupid elf and lunges forward in an attempt to separate your head from your shoulders. Its body stretches out in a sharp angle.

You sidestep quickly. The battleaxe whistles harmlessly through the space where you were standing. With all your strength, you rise up behind the bugbear and thrust your sword through its body.

When you are sure the bugbear is dead, you pull its body to the side of the room and cover it with a pile of weapons. You hurry to leave the room before someone arrives to investigate the sounds of the fight.

"Mrf, glub, glub." mumbles Mim.

You pick Mim up and hold it before your face. "If you promise to be helpful, I'll take the gag out." Slowly, you pull the gag out of Mim's mouth, expecting a tantrum. But Mim only sighs loudly and retreats into sulky silence.

There are two corridors to choose from. One goes left and the other right.

1. If you want to take the corridor going left, turn to page 115.
2. If you want to take the corridor going right, turn to page 142.

You slip a goblin cloak and helmet over your clothes and slip into the right hand corridor.

"Good for you," Mim says. "You see, planning ahead is a good idea."

Please turn to page 150.

Hoping to pass as a goblin, you put your head down and march across the room toward the next corridor. "Good, Lars," you mutter and keep on going. The wolves whine nervously and sniff the air. As you pass by them and near the corridor, you break into a run. Your scent carries to the cave wolves. They realize you are not a goblin! Before you can take four more steps, they fall on you and eat you. Now your father will never know what happened to you or his kingdom.

"I could have told him about the wolves," moans Mim. "But he wouldn't give me a chance to talk."

A wolf trots over and picks Mim up in its jaws and strolls off into the darkness.

The End...
of this adventure. Go back to the beginning and choose again.

You find yourself in a small room where many pieces of clothing and armor hang from pegs on the wall. It's a cloakroom!

Suddenly there is the tramp of many feet. You look out of the cloak room and see a band of goblins dressed in cloaks and helmets hurrying along the corridor toward an orc guard standing at another door down the corridor.

"Advance and identify yourselves," demands the orc guard.

"Telmac, Chief of the Polager Clan," answers the goblin chief.

The last of the goblins passes your doorway. A dangerous plan comes to your mind.

You place a horned goblin helmet on your head. It covers your ears and part of your forehead. You tuck your blonde hair down inside the hood of your cloak. If you are not closely examined, you can pass for a goblin. Strapping a wooden shield on your left arm and grasping your sword in your right hand, you try to bolster your courage for the deadly charade.

Should you take the risk and try to pass yourself off as a goblin? Yes! Quietly, you join the end of the goblin column.

"We're off to the meeting. Stand aside! We're late," says Telmac.

Turn to page 113.

The straight corridor is lit at intervals by torches. You notice that the walls have been greatly damaged and that now they are braced with wooden beams. There are signs of a battle. You wonder what could have caused the terrible damage. What could terrify orcs, goblins and gnolls so much that they are working together against a common enemy?

The corridor opens to an enormous cavern. The roof of the cavern flickers in the red light of many torches. Stalagmites and stalactites rise and descend out of the gloom like huge teeth. Centuries of dripping mineral water have created this glittering crystal room. Once it was your father's ballroom and meeting hall. Your happy memories of those days are shattered by the presence of the evil monsters who now fill the cavern.

Moving like a shadow, you hide behind a stalactite.

At the back wall of the cavern, a fossilized waterfall hangs in frozen space. Your father's throne still sits on the crest of the stone wave. Suddenly a rat scampers toward the throne and leaps on the seat.

When your father ruled, rats were hunted with weasels and dogs and destroyed. There were no rats in your father's kingdom. Now, this foul creature sits on your father's throne before its kingdom of monsters.

What can be happening? As you watch, the rat starts to grow. First, it is the size of a large rat... then a cat... then a dog... then a sheep. Then incredibly, it is man-sized. As it grows, an even more horrifying change takes place. The rat's body changes to that of a heavily muscled six-foot tall man, but it still bears the tail, fur and evil face of a rat. It's a wererat!

The wererat leans forward and stares wickedly at the crowd of monsters, resting its weight on the point of a razor sharp sword. Thrown over its shoulders is a magnificient cloak of silver gray fur.

Its red eyes and white fangs gleam evilly in the torchlight. You try to remember all you know about wererats. You know that wererats can take the form of giant rats, man-sized rat men, or full sized normal humans. They are evil, powerful and can command the obedience of all the monsters in the room.

By sheer force of its wicked stare, the wererat quiets the noisy crowd. Even after the mob of monsters is silent, it continues to stare grimly at them. You know the monsters are afraid and that they will obey and follow the wererat without question.

In a chilling whisper, the wererat begins to speak, "Most of you know me. I am Frang...Frang, Render of Flesh. I am your leader because I have defeated all enemies. If I order it, you will die for me."

Frang whispers on, "A new and deadly enemy invades our territory. None alive knows what it is for none has survived its attack. Whatever or whomever it is, it can burrow through solid stone and earth walls.

"The invader crushes barricades like eggshells. Whole patrols have disappeared leaving behind only some shattered armor and pools of blood as evidence that they existed.

"We do not fear elves, men, or each other. All are enemies we have faced before and can face again. This new enemy must be met by all of us. Until it is found and destroyed, we must all cooperate. If we fight each other, we will be lost."

Frang lets its words sink in, then asks in its hissing whisper, "Are there any here who oppose me?"

No one answers him.

"Then, I command," Frang whispers. "Be alert. Be ruthless. Show no mercy. This is our kingdom. We fought for it and won. Should you find any who are not of us, ask no question, kill them instantly. The slayer of the unknown invader will be made my second in command. So be it. Frang has spoken."

With one last cold glance at the monsters, Frang rises from the throne and strides away.

You stay hidden until the hall begins to bustle with monsters discussing the fearful Frang and its message.

When the hall is crowded with figures, you move to the passageway leading out of the cavern. Most of the monsters are dressed as you and are deep in conversation You attract no attention.

Stumbling along the corridor, you are filled with fear of Frang. You wonder about all you have heard about the unknown invader.

Moving slowly along the corridor, you see others, with duties to attend to, hurrying ahead of you. You are the last in the echoing corridor. Ahead of you, the corridor divides into two branches, one going left and the other going right. "Which way should we go?" you whisper to Mim.

"How about straight home?" replies Mim in a worried voice.

1. If you choose the left corridor, turn to page 120.
2. If you choose the corridor going right, turn to page 126.

"Listen, I got orders. Everybody who goes through here gets checked out. We've got an elf loose down here. So I don't care if you tell me you're Frang's mother, I have to check you out."

Telmac snarls and says, "Remember who you're talking to. We Polagers take no insults. If you're smart, you won't be here when we get back from the meeting." The goblins move out and you follow along at the back of the column.

The orc guard glares at you but you tuck your chin down and follow close on the heels of the goblin ahead of you.

Heart pounding, you pass it and enter another corridor. Fearing that other guards might be posted, you decide to follow the goblin column. You lag behind but stay close enough to rejoin the column, if necessary. Thankfully, Mim stays quiet.

Turn to page 107.

Holding your torch above your head, you grasp your sword. You enter the room at a dead run, screaming at the top of your lungs.

Rising up, the gnoll sees you coming. Your sword is pointed straight at its heart. It runs out a doorway on the other side of the room, begging, "Please don't hurt me." Still crying, it disappears down the corridor.

"Well!" says Mim," I guess we showed that monster. "Boo!" Mim tries to scare the salamander who looks at you with a bored expression and walks slowly away.

"Please excuse that lapse of behavior. I really got carried away," says Mim. "Now, I suggest we take a look around and see what remains of your father's treasures."

Pleased with your success, you follow Mim's advice and go through the doorway on the far side of the room and out into the corridor.

Please turn to page 55.

Black water drips continuously from the walls and ceiling in the corridor. The water on the floor is ankle deep. A strong breeze blows, making it difficult to keep your torch lit. The air is damp and uncomfortable. You clutch your cloak closely around you and splash onward.

The corridor winds on endlessly. Cold and miserable, you are wet to the waist. Your torch flickers and dies. Heaving a sigh, you tuck it in your belt. Your elven-sight reveals nothing but water and walls but you hear a distant roaring noise.

The stream deepens and the current increases. You are swept off your feet and are thrown against a pile of boulders. You are pinned against the rocks for a long time as the black water swirls around you. Finally, the current heaves you over the rocks. You feel a great rush of speed and then you start to fall.

You land in a large pool and water pours down over your head from above. You tread water desperately trying to stay afloat.

After a short time, you hear a sneeze.

"Rotten cave," says something very close to you.

There is a cough and a choke, "Blarf!" croaks a tiny voice.

Quickly you wrap a handful of your cloak around Mim. This is the wrong time for Mim to start to talk. You hear some muffled muttering but you squeeze Mim tightly and soon it is quiet.

Listening carefully, you hear a sound like stones being rubbed together. There is another sneeze, more muttering and more soft rubbing. Finally, a small spark appears. A tiny flame erupts and between sneezes is coaxed into a small fire.

In the firelight, you see a young kobold hunched over the fire trying to warm itself. Its skin is a scaly gray-brown and it has no hair. A bumpy crest runs between two nubby horns on its head. It has large bat-like ears, red eyes and a dog-like muzzle filled with sharp teeth.

Creeping to the water's edge, you watch it from the safety of a large boulder. It shivers over a fire made of old, dry bones. It is snuffling, sneezing and coughing. Will the cold weaken the kobold, you wonder, or will it only make the kobold meaner and nastier?

Looking past the kobold, you see that the cave has an exit off into the darkness. You don't know where it leads, but at least the ground looks dry.

1. If you want to attack the kobold, turn to page 33.
2. If you want to paddle quietly back out into the stream and drift with the current, turn to page 34.

There are two dark tunnels at the foot of the rockfall, one going left, the other, right. Looking and listening carefully, you can see a green glow at the end of the right tunnel. You can hear a deep rumble coming from the left tunnel.

"Don't just stand there. Make a choice," grumbles Mimulus. "As I suggested before, let's go home."

You pick the amulet up off your chest, look at it, and say, "We have to go on. I promised my father."

"I just knew you'd say that," sighs Mimulus. "Well, your choices don't look too good to me.

1. "Do you want to turn left, toward that green glow?" Turn to page 15.
2. "Or do we go to the right, toward that nasty rumbling sound?" Turn to page 71.

Reluctantly, with one hand on your sword, you enter the darkened corridor and edge along the walls. Even with your elvensight, you can barely see your hand in front of your face. A glittering dust fills the air, making your elvensight almost useless. The noise of the orcs can still be heard. Snatches of their talk and song drift back to you.

Barely able to see, you stumble over a boulder. Your head is spinning and you sit down to catch your breath. After a while, rubbing skinned nose and bruised knees, you hobble off into the glittering dust.

The last of the orc noises disappear. You are all alone in the corridor. You think of your father waiting for you to return with news of his lost kingdom. Tears fill your eyes. You wonder if you will ever see your family again. Filled with gloomy thoughts, you turn a corner and face a frightening sight.

Sitting in the remains of an orc guard room is the biggest, most terrifying weasel you have ever seen. He is eight feet long from his shell pink nose to the end of his silvery tail. The weasel is splattered with blood. Dead orcs litter the room. As you watch, the weasel uses his delicate paws to stuff most of a dead orc into his mouth. A great splintering, crunching sound fills the room.

After polishing off most of the orcs, the weasel settles down to groom himself like an ordinary house cat. You cannot help but compare him to a pet weasel, named Sissel, you had as a child.

As the weasel finishes his grooming and stands on his hind legs, you see an amazing sight...he has a star-shaped patch on his chest just like Sissel. Could it be? Is it possible? Hope and excitement fill your heart.

When Brookmere was overrun, Sissel and his brothers and sisters were already about three feet high. Even then they were well trained to follow your commands. Often they shared your childhood adventures.

Thinking of Sissel reminds you of his mother, Strina, a favored pet of your household. Due to her great age, she spent most of her time lying in front of the fire in Brookmere's great kitchen. A lump rises in your throat as you remember the bedtime stories she often told you.

How often you have wondered about the fate of your beloved pets, lost when the castle fell.

The giant weasel's nose starts to quiver as he lifts his head and sniffs the air. He turns swiftly to face you and opens his fearsome mouth full of needle-sharp teeth. He starts to leap at you, thinking you are a goblin from the scent of the goblin cloak you wear.

"I say, youngster, do you think you can do something to prevent our becoming dessert?" asks Mim.

You waste no time talking but throw the cloak off and step forward. Perhaps it is a foolish move? If the weasel is not Sissel, you will surely be eaten, but it is your only hope.

If he is Sissel, will he still recognize you?

"Sissel," you call. "It is I, Brion. Remember the days of our friendship here in Brookmere? Remember the love we felt for one another? Do not attack!"

"If only I had fingers to cross!" moans Mim.

Slowly the killing fury fades from the weasel's eyes. Sniffing intently, he steps toward you approaching until his huge head is only inches away from you. His shell pink nose sniffs all parts of your body, separating your true scent from the goblin scent that clings to your clothes.

Emitting a squeal of joy, the weasel nuzzles his huge head into your chest. He is Sissel! He rolls over on his back baring his stomach for you to rub as you did in the old days. After a few minutes, he leaps to his feet, his body trembling with excitement.

"What a touching scene," says Mim.

When you are able to stop Sissel from joyously licking your face, you convince him to tell you his story.

"When Brookmere fell," says Sissel, "I was off hunting with my brothers and sisters. When we returned, we found all we loved destroyed. Our grief turned to rage when we discovered that the monsters had killed Strina, our mother. The pelt that Frang, Render of Flesh wears as a cloak is that of our mother.

"Since that day, my family and I have avenged her death by killing as many monsters as possible. We know many tunnels the monsters have not yet found. We go through these tunnels until we find rooms filled with monsters. Then, we weaken the walls from behind, break through and kill all in sight. None have survived such an attack but neither have we caught Frang."

You tell Sissel your story and about Frang's meeting. You decide that it would be best to leave the dungeon quickly and return home. When you return home, you will tell your father the story. Sissel will retreat and gather his brothers and sisters into an army. Together with the weasels attacking from inside and your father's army waiting outside, there will be no escape for the monsters. Brookmere will be yours once again.

"A masterful plan," cries Mim. "A touch of genius. One would think it was my idea!"

Please turn to page 136.

You follow the end of the goblin column down the poorly lit corridor. They move swiftly talking among themselves. You overhear small snatches of their conversation. They are worried about the unknown invader and are afraid of being ambushed. They hurry toward the safety of the well-lit room where there will be other goblins.

The goblins turn a corner. You hear them say, "Good, Lars. Down, Lothar. Stop licking me Fritz." Then there is only silence.

You wait for a minute to make sure they are gone. You think that Lars, Lothar and Fritz must be harmless pets so you turn the corner and walk into the room.

"Might I suggest..." begins Mim in a worried voice. You do not stop to listen.

Lars, Lothar, and Fritz are cave wolves. Each stands about six feet high at the shoulders and is a silvery gray color. An elf is a tasty bite for one of them. Now, all three of them are eying you as though you are about to become their mid-afternoon snack.

1. If you want to try to talk to them with Mim's aid, turn to page 31.
2. If you want to run away down the corridor ahead of you, turn to page 105.
3. If you want to try to fight the cave wolves, turn to page 145.

Swords and daggers did the orcs little good against the gelatinous cube. You strike once, twice, three times. You manage to slice out several sections before it is on you. Then, you are gripped with intense pain. Your body burns all over. Dropping your sword, you try to run.

"Why didn't you listen to me?" says Mim. "Sometimes it doesn't pay to fight." Mim laspes into silence.

You are in terrible pain and pay Mim no attention. Greatly reduced in size, but still dangerous, the gelatinous cube now lies quietly pulsing in the center of the room.

Staggering out of the left hand door, you find yourself breathing fresh air. A corridor leads you outside of your ruined kingdom. Delirious with pain, you collapse on the ground.

130

You are found by a band of hunters to whom Mim tells your story.

The hunters bandage your wounds and return you to your father. You are ill for a long time with a high fever, lasping in and out of consciousness.

Mim tells your story to the entire kingdom. You are made a national hero.

Mim makes sure that it is an important part of your story and your father proclaims Mim a hero. A special holiday is held in its honor.

It will take a long time for you to recover. When you do, a new battle will be planned based on your information. Your father's kingdom will be taken from the monsters and will return to its former glory.

The End...

of this adventure. Go back to the beginning and choose again.

You decide not to fight the young goblin. The frightening words of its song convince you that it would rather have you for lunch than the fungus.

"Psst," hisses Mim softly. "I don't know your feeling on this but I do not wish to become a goblin's lunch. May I suggest we lie low until it finishes eating?"

You murmur in agreement and watching from behind the boulder, you settle down to wait.

Finally, the goblin finishes eating, picks up its club and shield and, still singing, strolls off into the tunnel.

After a few minutes, you feel safe enough to creep out from behind the stone. You sneak through the cavern watching for other goblins. You continue on. The corridor is straight and dry. You do not light your torch. Your elvensight reveals no monsters in this corridor.

The corridor bears evidence of the invading monsters. Once well tended, it is now full of bones and pieces of rusty armor, serving to remind you that the hard won victory was not yours.

The tunnel branches before you. The branch to your right leads back to the entrance. The branch to your left leads to the interior of the dungeon.

You look around the corner and down the left corridor and see two orcs holding spears and wearing leather armor and swords. They face a room and cannot see you nor can you see the room they are guarding.

"What do you think, Mim? Which way should we go?" you whisper.

"Why don't you ask me something simple like why is a raven like a writing desk?" snaps Mim. "If I knew the answer to your question, I'd be an oracle not an amulet."

You sigh unhappily. "Remind me to thank my father for giving you to me. Maybe he was trying to teach me patience."

"If you constantly rely on me," Mim says, "how will you ever develop any skills of your own? I'm here to help, not to lead."

What Mim says is true. Angry as you are, you do understand what it is trying to do. In an uneasy truce, the two of you continue on.

1. If you choose not to fight the orcs but to go back to the entrance and leave, turn to page 12.
2. If you want to attack the orcs, turn to page 40.

Knowing that swords and daggers did not help the orcs against the cube, you hold your torch to the edge of it. It grows smaller but suddenly it swings its bulk toward you and advances. You retreat to the door. As you hold the door with one hand and start to take another swing at it, it reaches you and delivers a painful blow that almost knocks you off your feet.

You drop your torch and close the door behind you. You collapse on the floor holding your arm. Your forearm, wrist, and hand are badly burned. It is difficult to move, and you are afraid you have lost the use of your hand forever.

"I almost did it," you mutter.

"Getting out alive is fine with me. You did well," says Mim proudly.

You are pleased to hear words of praise from Mim. Taking a lit torch from the wall, you walk slowly down the corridor.

A breath of fresh cool air blows against your face. You lean on the wall and gather your strength for one final effort.

"Come on. You can do it! Don't give up!" Mim urges.

You stagger on. At last you stumble outside and find yourself on a hillside covered with green grass, tall trees and wildflowers. In the valley below, you see shepherds tending their flocks. You call to them. They take you to their camp and nurse you back to health. When you regain your strength, you bid your new friends farewell and start out for home.

The kingdom honors your return with a great banquet. You tell your father all you have learned. Mim interrupts you constantly but it no longer bothers you. Armed with the information you have brought back, your father's fighters start to prepare for war. Soon they will march on Brookmere and it will be yours again!

The End...

of this adventure. Go back to the beginning and choose again.

Happily you walk down the corridor. Sissel has given you directions out of the dungeon. There will be guards to get past, but you are sure your luck will hold.

Approaching a room, you hear pacing. Looking around the corner of the door into the room, you see six kobolds.

Even though they are only three feet tall, kobolds are dangerous enemies. Their rusty brown skins are leather tough. They have no hair but sport small, nasty, pointed horns on their heads.

Dressed in leather armor and carrying swords, all six kobolds are marching stiffly back and forth across the room.

Two doors stand on the opposite end of the room.

1. If you choose to try and fool the kobolds with your goblin disguise, turn to page 10.
2. If you choose to fight the kobolds, turn to page 67.

Instead of answering the giant, you grasp your sword and swing it with all your strength down on its warty nose.

"Hey!" says the giant. "Not nice." It throws you against the stone wall with great force. Your head slams against the wall and you lose consciousness.

"What this?" says the giant as it rips Mim from around your neck.

"Put me down!" demands Mim.

"Hey, it talks. Neat!" says the happy giant. It drapes Mim on its forehead like a headband and walks off into the darkness.

When you awaken later, you cannot remember who you are or why you are sitting in a damp, dark place. All you know is that your head hurts.

You may never know the answers. You wander out the door. You may survive. If you do, you may remember your mission and all you have learned. Then again, you may not...

The End...
of this adventure. Go back to the beginning and choose again.

The giant is still holding you firmly by the neck of your tunic. You are gasping for breath and your head pounds.

"I'm a friend of Furd's," you say, hoping the giant hasn't spoken to Furd recently.

"Oh, yeah?" says the giant. "Furd my brother but me smarter. If you friend of Furd, why you here?"

"I just helped Furd win a game of boulder bowling from Ool and I'm on my way home. I seem to be lost. Could you show me the way out of here?"

"Well, guess so, if you friend of Furd." says the giant.

"Sure I am," you force a chuckle from your dry throat. "We could go ask. Furd will tell you I'm a good friend."

Crossing your fingers, you hope the giant doesn't take you up on your offer.

"No, too far to walk. Believe you. That door go out over there. You better be telling the truth or you be very sorry."

The giant puts you back on the ground and points you to the door on the right side of the room.

"Goodbye. Thank you." you say, meaning it from the bottom of your heart.

You open a door and step into another corridor. Fresh air blows on your face and you smell the green smell of things growing. Soon you will be above ground and among friends once again.

You are happy. You will soon be able to tell your father all you have learned. With his forces, Brookmere will be yours again.

The End...
of this adventure. Go back to the beginning and choose again.

You speed along the corridor until you see a brightly lit room ahead of you. "Halt!" demands an orcish voice. "Advance and state your name and business."

At first you think the orc is speaking to you but then you hear a voice saying, "Tong of the Daxid Clan going to the meeting.

"Pass," says the first voice. "Get a move on, you're late."

Creeping closer, you are suddenly surrounded by heavy folds of material carrying the foul smell of goblin.

You strike out in terror and swing around wildly until you realize your attacker is a cloak. You have wandered into a goblin cloakroom and are fighting a goblin cloak.

You see rows of cloaks, boots, helmets and a pile of neatly stacked weapons.

Knowing an elf stands no chance of passing the orc guard ahead of you, you try to think of a plan.

"Okay, I'll give you one more chance. What do you think I should do now?" you ask Mim.

"A simple matter," says Mim, "remember, when in Argoria, do as the Agorians do."

"Terrific, I ask for answers and you give me riddles. You're no help."

Mim's words do make you think. You start to see what it was getting at. You should disguise yourself as a goblin.

1. If you want to put on a goblin cloak and try the corridor on the right, turn to page 104.

2. If you want to put on a goblin cloak and try to fool the orc guard and follow the corridor straight ahead, turn to page 150.

You move happily down the corridor. Wearing your goblin disguise, you walk into the room and draw your sword. "Hello, Lars. Hello, Lothar. Hello, Fritz," you say and continue into the room.

The cave wolves are puzzled. They see and smell goblin but something isn't right. By the time they catch the scent of elf, you are among them swinging your sword and have killed the nearest wolf. The two remaining wolves become a mass of snarling fangs and teeth. You battle long and hard. The wolves work together as a team trying to rip and tear you apart from both sides at once. Finally, one moves too close and you strike it a fatal blow. Turning quickly, you manage to kill the last wolf. You have not escaped the battle unhurt. Your arms and legs are slashed and are bleeding heavily... but you have won!

Working quickly, you pull the wolves to the far corner of the room and mop up their blood with some rags you find in the room. You hope the orcs don't find the bodies of their pets until you can get far away.

"Masterfully done, Brion," cries Mim. "I'm proud of you."

146

You feel that you have been in the dark corridors forever. More than anything, you want to be outside with the cool fresh wind blowing in your face. But all you see ahead are endless tunnels and darkness. You want to quit and go home but you have given your word. More than just your pride is at stake, you must keep going if you are to survive.

Out of nowhere, you hear singing. You can't make out the words but you decide to try to trace the sound to its source. You sneak close, curious but careful.

You peep around the corner into a torchlit room. The torches are nearly burned out.

Three large drunken gnolls slump against the far wall sharing the contents of a wine skin.

"You know, Hodge," says the first gnoll, "We could get into big trouble for this. We're supposed to be on guard duty."

"We are on guard, Deiter," says Hodge. "We're guarding the wall over there." All three gnolls fall over laughing at the joke.

"Now I'm guarding the ceiling," says Hodge laughing foolishly.

Deiter finishes the wine and put the opening of the wine skin to its eye. "Look, Hodge, Rifkin, I'm guarding the wine skin. The wine's all gone!"

"Oh no!" cries Rifkin, the third gnoll. "Can we get some more?"

"No, someone would see us," says Deiter.

"We could go to sleep," says Hodge, curling up in a ball.

"No," says Rifkin kicking him.

"Stop it, both of you. Remember, we're on guard duty," says Deiter swaying slightly.

Groaning, all three stumble to their feet. They weave across the room in a drunken imitation of guard duty, tripping occasionally.

Suddenly, all three collide with a clash of armor and fall to the floor in a tangle of arms, legs, and spears.

"May I suggest," whispers Mim "that you seize the opportunity to present these drunken monsters with some sort of permanent injury?"

"You don't mean kill them, do you?" you whisper.

"Youngster, you have grasped the essence of the situation," says Mim.

Turn to page 22.

Wrapped from head to toe in the goblin cloak, you creep down the corridor feeling safe. Thanks to the cloak, you both look and smell like a goblin. If necessary, you can fool the guards.

You look around a corner and before you stands an orc guard mumbling to itself, "Talk to me like that! Who do they think they are? A bunch of crummy goblins, that's all. If they come back here, I'll teach them a lesson. I'll rip off their noses. Not even a goblin from Clan Daxid can talk to Swart like that." The orc guard continues to mumble on to itself.

Swart guards the only way out. Unless you want to go back, you must think of some way of getting around it. A strange idea comes to mind. It's so strange that it jus might work. You pull the goblin cloak around your face and walk into the room.

Knees knocking with fear, you say, "Excuse me, Mr. Swart. I was sent by my clan to apologize for any harsh words.

"We hope you did not take offense as none was intended. We do not want any hard feelings. We know you were just doing your job. Everyone knows how well you do your job. We know you would never let any personal feelings interfere with your job. I was sent back to make sure you know how much we respect you and hope you will forgive us."

With its mouth gaping open, Swart stares at you, "Are you kidding me?" It squints its piggy eyes at you. "You heard about me?"

"Oh, surely," you say quickly. "Why, everyone has heard of you Swart, the best guard around.

"Well, I guess I am. You better hurry along or you'll be late for the meeting. Hurry up now. Catch up with the others. I have to get back to my guarding."

Swart snaps to attention and starts to strut back and forth as you hurry through the room to the tunnel. You smile to yourself wondering how long it will take Swart to realize you came from the wrong direction. Now you know there are goblins ahead of you. You must move carefully so you do not run into them.

Please turn to page 107.

ENDLESS QUEST™ Books

Ask for these exciting DUNGEONS & DRAGONS™ titles at better bookstores and hobby shops everywhere!

#1 DUNGEON OF DREAD

You are a fighter in quest of treasure, willing to challenge the evil wizard in his mountain hideaway. Only by quick thinking and action will you emerge safely from the Dungeons of Dread.

#2 MOUNTAIN OF MIRRORS

An elven warrior hoping to keep your village from starving, you must enter the mysterious Mountain of Mirrors to fight monsters who have been stealing caravans of food.

#3 PILLARS OF PENTEGARN

You and your friends, Fox and Owl, journey into the ruins of Castle Pentegarn. You join three adventurers who are after the powerful Staff of Kings.

#4 RETURN TO BROOKMERE

You are an elven prince who must return to the ruins of the family castle, Brookmere, and learn what evil lurks there. Only courage and cleverness will bring you out.

#5 REVOLT OF THE DWARVES

The dwarves who once served your kingdom have revolted. You and your family are the first humans to be captured. But you escape! You must warn the prince and save your family.

#6 REVENGE OF THE RAINBOW DRAGONS

You are Jaimie, wizard apprentice to Pentegarn, on quest to Rainbow Castle to meet the challenge of three evil wizards. You must use wits and courage to save yourself.

For a free catalog write:
TSR Hobbies, Inc.
POB 756 Dept. EQB
Lake Geneva, WI 53147